THE UNKNOWN PLANET

Read about the amazing space adventures of Finn, Shimma and their friends in this gripping sci-fi fantasy.

Jean Ure was six when she wrote her first book and still at school when her first novel was published. Since then, she has written many popular titles for young people, including *A Proper Little Nooryeff, Hi There, Supermouse* and *Plague 99* (1991 Lancashire Children's Book of the Year). She is the author of three other Walker titles for young readers, *The Wizard in the Woods, The Wizard in Wonderland* and *Captain Cranko and the Crybaby*. Jean Ure lives in Croydon, Surrey with her husband, five dogs and two cats.

Some other titles

Art, You're Magic!
by Sam McBratney

Jolly Roger
by Colin McNaughton

Pappy Mashy
by Kathy Henderson

The Snow Maze
by Jan Mark

Tillie McGillie's Fantastical Chair
by Vivian French

JEAN URE
THE UNKNOWN PLANET

Illustrations by
Chris Winn

WALKER BOOKS
LONDON

For Alex and Rosie
C.W.

First published 1992 by Walker Books Ltd
87 Vauxhall Walk, London SE11 5HJ

This edition published 1994

2 4 6 8 10 9 7 5 3 1

Text © 1992 Jean Ure
Illustrations © 1992 Chris Winn

Printed in England by Clays Ltd, St Ives plc

British Library Cataloguing in Publication Data
A catalogue record for this book is
available from the British Library.

ISBN 0-7445-3102-0

Contents

Alarm!
9

Crash
21

Time Runs Out
35

Saved!
49

Alarm!

Shimma was practising aquabatics
in the children's pool when the
alarm went off – *peep peep peep!*

It could be heard all over the ship. Almost immediately, the Captain's voice came over the loud speaker. "Spaceship *Sea Queen*! This is an emergency. Will all passengers please get into their spacesuits and assemble on the top deck. I repeat –"

Shimma didn't wait. With one quick flip she was across the pool and diving head first through the hatch into the main body of the ship. Finn! She must find Finn!

"Shimma!"

A figure in a spacesuit loomed before her.

"F-Finn?"

All the lights had gone out and in the dark it was difficult to tell.

"Here – quick!"

It *was* Finn! He had fetched her
spacesuit and now, with clumsy
haste, he helped her into it. All
around them, in the murky gloom,
other spacesuited figures bumped
and jostled.

The alarm continued its high-pitched squeal – *peep peep peep!* And all the time, the Captain's voice could be heard, urgently repeating its message.

"Spaceship
Sea Queen! This
is an emergency! … "
Together, Finn and Shimma
fought their way up to the top deck.

15

It was crowded with anxious figures, moon-headed in their space helmets. Finn and Shimma stayed close together, Finn with both arms wrapped protectively about his sister. The Captain's voice came again over the loud speaker.

"May I have your attention, please! We are about to make an emergency landing. Will all passengers take their places in the safety capsules. The planet we are about to land on has not been charted. We do not yet know whether it is life supporting."

Huddled against Finn in capsule number three, Shimma tried hard to pretend that all this was just make-believe. It couldn't really be happening!

Three months ago, the *Sea Queen* had launched into space from the planet Aqua. Aqua was dying; its seas were drying up, its lush greenery turning to desert. A new home was needed, and was needed fast. The *Sea Queen*, with its crew

of twelve and its fifty children, was
one of a whole fleet of ships which
had been sent out, all of them
seeking the safety of the warm wet
worlds which lay on the far side
of space.

Now the fleet sailed on, leaving their sister ship behind to face the perils of the unknown planet…

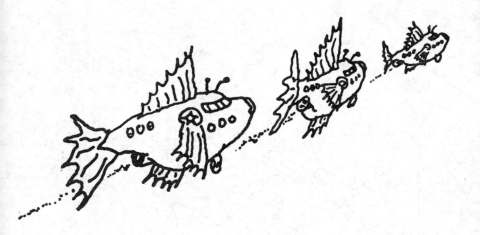

Crash

Shimma's head felt as though it were bursting. Through the porthole she could see stars whizzing and whirling, making dizzying patterns in the sky.

The ship was spinning, out of control. Over and over, it tumbled through space.

The next minute and – CRASH!
The whole ship juddered as it hit
something hard. At the same time
came the shrill screaming of the
hooter – *aahwaaa, aahwaaa,
aahwaaa!* Everyone knew what
that meant: danger! abandon ship!

With shaking hands, Shimma
fumbled for the clasp which would
release her. She felt herself jerked
upright by Finn and bundled
towards the exit. Already
the emergency
hatches were
sliding
open.

When Shimma's turn came, Finn
squeezed her hand and sent her off
ahead of him. It happened so
quickly she hardly had time
to be scared. No sooner
had she shot down
the escape tube
and out at the
other end
than Finn
appeared
by her
side.

The passengers and crew of the
stricken *Sea Queen* stood huddled
together for comfort. The lights

26

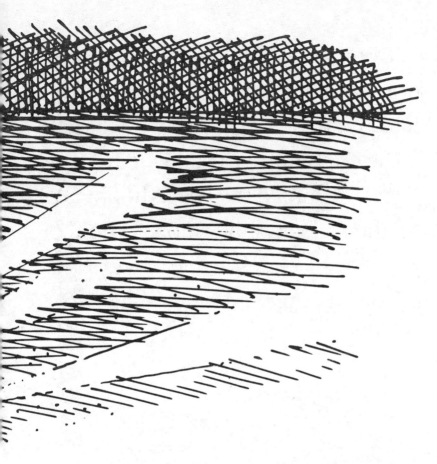

from their helmets showed that the
ship had landed on a vast expanse
of rock, flat and bare as far as the
eye could see. Shimma reached out
for Finn's hand.

"Don't worry," he said. "They'll soon have her working again. We shan't be here long."

The Captain was just giving his orders – "Unload the space-hoppers! Get them clear of the ship" – when out of the blackness came a loud and hideous roaring and the ground began to tremble at their feet.

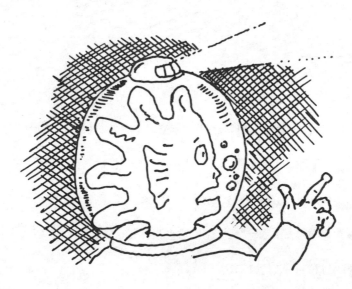

Even as they stood there, not
knowing which way to run for
safety, the thing leapt at them. Over
the rim of the rocky plateau it came,
snorting and bellowing, jaws gaping
wide, yellow eyes glowing like twin
suns in the darkness.

The spitting and hissing of the monster mingled with the terrified screams of its victims. Shimma saw a snarling mouth, with rows of teeth, plunging straight at her. She had just time to glimpse the huge padded feet before a blast of hot air flung her to the ground.

Shimma lay for a few seconds,
not daring to move.

She felt people trampling over her in
their panic to get away. Then she felt
someone shake her by the shoulder
and say urgently, "Shimma!"

"Finn!"

They clung to each other. The
monster had gone, raging and
bellowing into the night. Behind it

lay a trail of devastation. Two crew
members had been badly mauled
and three of the ship's space-
hoppers had been wrecked.

But worst of all was the *Sea
Queen* – she lay in a tangled heap,
damaged beyond all hope of repair.

They were prisoners of the
unknown planet!

Time Runs Out

The Captain called everyone
together. He addressed them,
bracingly. "All is not lost," he told
them. "The whole of the planet
cannot be made of bare rock. We
must set out to explore – and we
must do it quickly, before another
of the monsters comes upon us."

But they had only one space-hopper left! How could they all get into one space-hopper?

The two wounded crew members would go in the space-hopper, said the Captain, together with the youngest of the children and Lieutenant Gill to take charge. The rest of them would have to rely on their jet-packs.

"I'm not going without Finn!"
cried Shimma.

Finn swallowed. "You must," he
said. "Be brave. You must go ahead
and find somewhere safe where
we can make a home."

The space-hopper set off across
the barren rock. Finn could see
Shimma, a small, forlorn figure,

sitting next to her friend Flip. She waved at him. With heavy heart, he waved back.

"Come," said the Captain, turning on his jet-pack. "Let us waste no time."

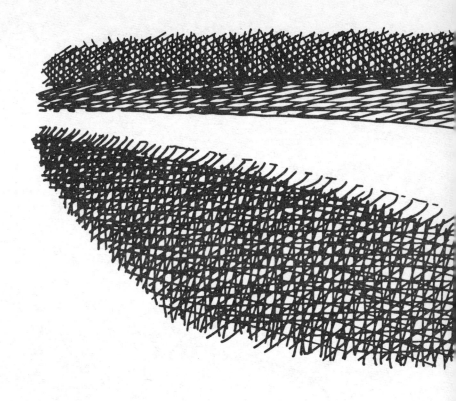

Across the rock they skimmed,
the Captain in the lead. Quite soon,
the space-hopper was out of sight.
Following in its path, they scudded
up a slope on to a strange white
plain, hard and shining.

What kind of planet was this?

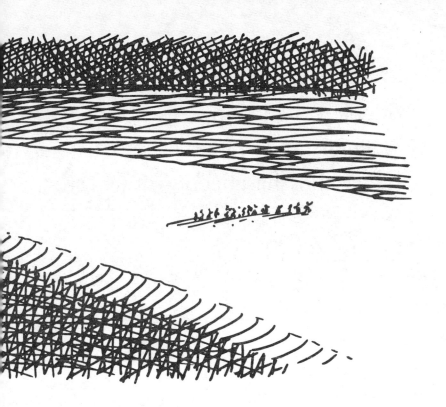

wondered Finn. Had it no water, no
grass, no trees?

Wearily they made their way
across the plain, only to find
themselves dipping down once
again on to more of the black rock.

Was there no end to it?

The Captain's personal intercom suddenly crackled into life. The Captain listened. At last! The message they had been waiting for!

Through his space-scope, Lieutenant Gill had spotted something which looked like a forest. Hearts lifted. So there *was* an end to it!

Shortly after that, the first streaks of an alien pink dawn crept into the sky and the forest became clear for all to see. A great cheer went up. Maybe they would find a place for themselves after all!

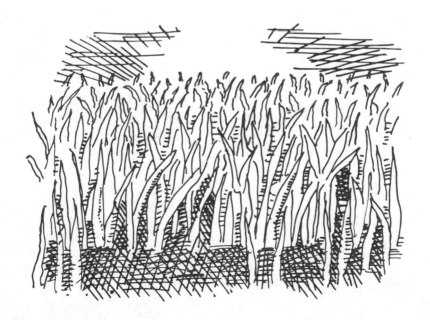

They had just reached the safety of the trees when they heard it again – **GRAAAARRRGH!** The spine-chilling cry of a monster.

"Quick!" shouted the Captain. "Take cover!"

Peering fearfully out from behind a stout tree trunk, Finn saw that in the distance the rocky platform was suddenly alive with the creatures, all leaping and roaring and belching hot breaths of smoke.

Luckily they seemed too intent on chasing one another to show any interest in the travellers.

"They are obviously rock dwellers,"
said the Captain, "and not forest
creatures. If we keep under cover
then perhaps we shall be safe."

They pushed on, as fast as they could, through green leafless trees which grew straight and tall without any branches. Spirits rose. Surely in a world where green things grew they would be able to make a home for themselves?

"So long as we find somewhere soon," muttered one of the crew members.

He would never have said it if he had known that Finn was listening; but Finn was not stupid. He had been in space long enough to know that for those outside the space-hopper, time would soon start running out…

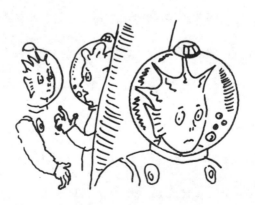

Saved!

The forest had given way to a wide stretch of desert. Spirits fell as quickly as they had risen: desert was not good.

They could see the space-hopper
ahead of them, rolling and rocking
in the soft sand. Space-hoppers
were not designed to go on sand.

The Captain spoke into his intercom. "Calling space-hopper! Do you need assistance? Over."

Lieutenant Gill never had the chance to reply. Before he could say a word an enormous white ball, half the size of a spaceship and

travelling very nearly as fast, had
come hurtling out of nowhere and
slammed broadside on into the
space-hopper.

The blast could be felt even at the edge of the desert.

Finn watched in horror as the space-hopper burst apart, sending a shower of small spacesuited figures whirling helplessly into the air. Even as he darted forward, an unseen wind was lifting them and carrying them high over the desert, towards a range of big black hills

in the distance. Another second, and they were gone.

"Shimma!" he shouted. "Shimma!"

He blundered on, into a cloud of sand. The Captain caught him just in time. Finn struggled, but he knew there was nothing he could do. There was nothing anyone could do. When the sand finally settled, all the spacesuited figures had gone…

Tear bubbles burst from Finn's eyes. Shimma! Oh, Shimma! The Captain bent his head. "They were brave adventurers," he said. They stood for a few moments in silence. The Captain placed a hand on Finn's shoulder. As he did so, the intercom crackled. The Captain listened. A strange expression stole over his face.

"That was Lieutenant Gill! Our friends are safe! They've landed in a place where we can settle! Let's go!"

Across the desert they raced,
guided by the voice of Lieutenant
Gill over the intercom. On the way
they passed the large white ball
which had so nearly caused disaster.

Could it be an asteroid?
wondered Finn.

The Captain said he thought it
very likely.

Now they had reached the range of hills, tall and forbidding, at the edge of the desert. They stood for a moment in dismay. Their air supplies were running out fast. They would never be able to make it all the way to the top!

Finn, in despair, stumbled and almost fell. It was then that he saw it – a far-off gleam of daylight between two hills.

"Through there!" He pointed.
Along the rocky tunnel they
staggered, giddy and weak for lack
of air. Slowly the gleam of light
came closer. Would they ever
manage to reach it?

Finn was the first to come tumbling out from the end of the tunnel. He blinked, his eyes dazzled by the sunlight.

There in front of him lay a shining sea; and bobbing in the water, bouncing on the waves, were Shimma and Flip and all the others!

"Shimma!" gasped Finn.

He tore off his spacesuit and helmet and dived in. Shimma and Flip swam joyously towards him, their scales glinting as they came through the water.

"We've discovered what this place is called!" cried Shimma. She broke surface and waved.

Finn turned his head to look.

SAFE BATHING, he read.

They would make a new home
for themselves in Safe Bathing!

MORE WALKER PAPERBACKS
For You to Enjoy

☐ 0-7445-3103-9 *Art, You're Magic*
               by Sam McBratney /
               Tony Blundell   £2.99

☐ 0-7445-3173-X *Jolly Roger*
               by Colin McNaughton   £2.99

☐ 0-7445-3096-2 *Pappy Mashy*
               by Kathy Henderson /
               Chris Fisher   £2.99

☐ 0-7445-3092-X *The Snow Maze*
               by Jan Mark / Jan Ormerod   £2.99

☐ 0-7445-3094-6 *Tillie McGillie's*
               Fantastical Chair
               by Vivian French / Sue Heap £2.99